Why I Love My Grandma

Illustrated by Daniel Howarth

HarperCollins *Children's Books*

I love my
grandma because...

she takes me for walks.

I love my grandma because...

she sings with me.

I love my
grandma because...

she lets me help her.

I love my grandma because...

we play hide-and-seek.

I love my
grandma because...

she likes to see the new
things I can do.

I love my grandma because...
she has me over to stay.

I love my
grandma because...

she kisses me.

I love my grandma because...

she cuddles me.

I love my
grandma because...

she carries me.

I love my
grandma because...

she knows
lots of things.

Everyone loves their grandma,

especially... ME!

First published in hardback in Great Britain by HarperCollins *Children's Books* in 2014
This edition published in 2020

1 3 5 7 9 10 8 6 4 2

978-0-00-798397-1

HarperCollins *Children's Books* is a division of HarperCollins*Publishers* Ltd.

Text and illustrations copyright © HarperCollins*Publishers* Ltd 2014

A CIP catalogue record for this title is available from the British Library.
Visit our website at: www.harpercollins.co.uk

Printed and bound in China